Published by Hachette Partworks Ltd.
ISBN: 978-1-908648-86-0
Date of Printing: October 2013
Printed in Malaysia by Tien Wah Press

DISNEY·PIXAR

MONSTERS, INC.

DISNEY·PIXAR

hachette

All children know that monsters come into their
bedrooms at night to scare them. But what they
don't know is that the monsters are only doing
their jobs. They collect children's screams and turn
them into electricity for the city of Monstropolis.

A huge, blue monster called Sulley was the top
Scarer at Monsters, Inc. His assistant was Mike.
Together they made a great team!

It was time for Sulley and Mike to go to work. On the Scare Floor was a row of doors, which led the monsters into children's bedrooms.

Randall was Sulley's biggest rival. He managed to collect lots of screams but by the end of the shift, Sulley had the most. He was still the best!

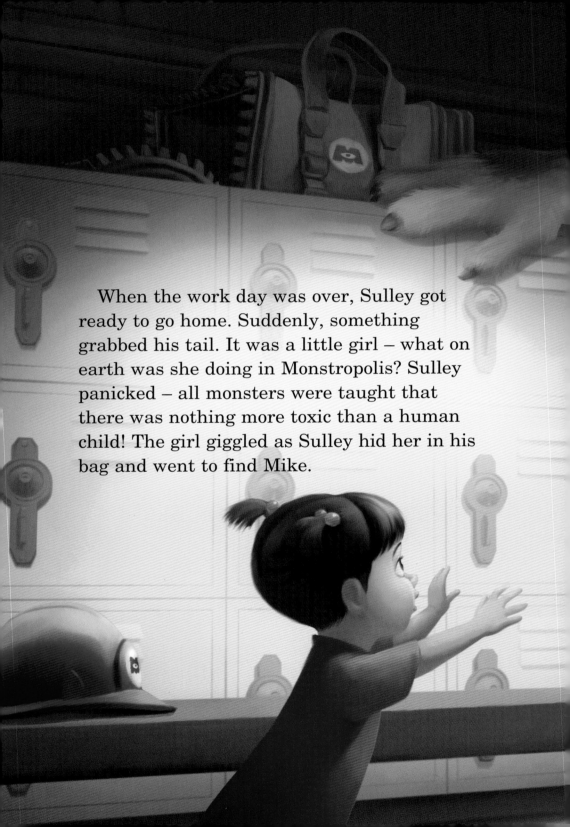

When the work day was over, Sulley got ready to go home. Suddenly, something grabbed his tail. It was a little girl – what on earth was she doing in Monstropolis? Sulley panicked – all monsters were taught that there was nothing more toxic than a human child! The girl giggled as Sulley hid her in his bag and went to find Mike.

Sulley found Mike at a restaurant, but while they were talking, the girl crept out of the bag. When they spotted her, the diners all screamed and ran away!

Mike and Sulley noticed something strange: whenever the girl laughed, all the lights came on. They managed to whisk the girl away before the security agents arrived.

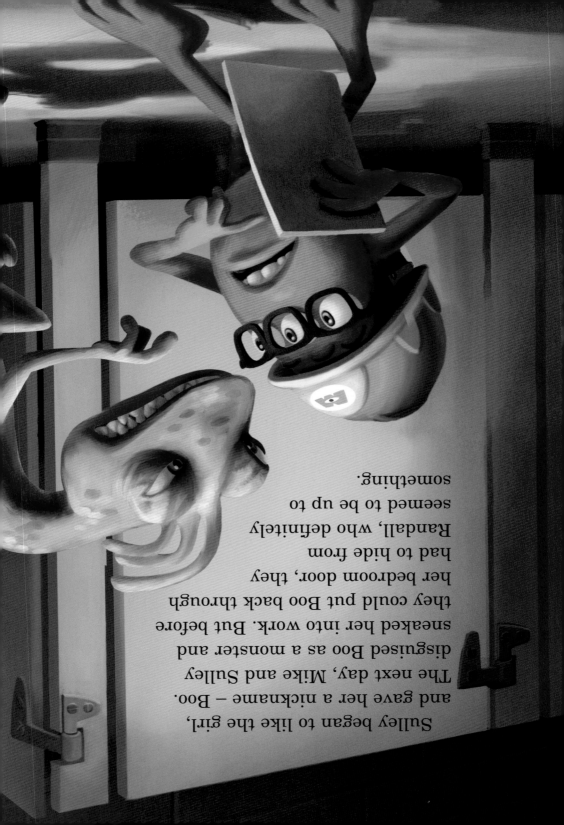

Sulley began to like the girl,
and gave her a nickname – Boo.
The next day, Mike and Sulley
disguised Boo as a monster and
sneaked her into work. But before
they could put Boo back through
her bedroom door, they
had to hide from
Randall, who definitely
seemed to be up to
something.

Randall had worked out that Mike and Sulley were hiding Boo. He told Mike that he would help them to get Boo home, but Sulley was suspicious. To prove everything was OK, Mike went through Boo's bedroom door first – but then he found himself trapped under a box!

Boo and Sulley followed Randall
to a secret lab, which had a machine
that sucked screams from a child.

Randall was furious when he saw Boo wasn't in
the box. He strapped Mike to the machine, but
Sulley and Boo rescued him. They all ran to ask Mr
Waternoose, the head of Monsters, Inc., for help.
But to their amazement, Waternoose grabbed Boo,
then pushed Mike and Sulley into the human world!

Waternoose strapped Boo into the
scream machine. Luckily, Sulley had
found a child's bedroom and managed
to get back to Monsters, Inc.

He crashed into the machine, making
it fall on Waternoose and his assistant,
Fungus. Sulley picked up Boo and ran.

But Randall was hot on their heels! Just then, Mike arrived in time to help his friend. Sulley had an idea. He told Mike to try to make Boo laugh. Her laughter immediately made all the doors on the Scare Floor open, so the three of them jumped in and out of the doors, hoping to shake Randall off.

At last, Randall managed to catch Boo. When Sulley went to help her, Randall attacked. Boo grabbed Randall's hair and pulled it, giving Sulley the chance to grab Randall and throw him into the human world, never to be seen again. Meanwhile, Mr Waternoose was arrested by the security agents.

It was time for Boo to go home.

"Nothing's going to scare you any more, is it?" said Sulley. Boo smiled. "Goodbye, Boo," he whispered. Then he quietly left the room, closing the door behind him.

Soon after, Sulley suggested turning the Scream
Floor into the Laugh Floor. Boo had shown him
that laughter was stronger than screams, so now
the monsters had a new job – making kids laugh!